Please Do Me Pregnant

An Erotic Story

Alexa Nichols

Quickies Series

C000124749

PLEASE DON'T GET ME PREGNANT!

QUICKIES SERIES

Copyright © 2016-2018 by Alexa Nichols

✉ alexa.nichols.author@gmail.com

🌐 http://alexanichols.com

f @AlexaNicholsAuthor

🐦 @AlexaNichols69

G+ alexa.nichols.author

t alexanicholsauthor

P alexanichols69

g alexanichols

Third Print Edition: August 2018

10 9 8 7 6 5 4 3 2 1

Contents...

Acknowledgements

I would like to dedicate this book to the Flying Spaghetti Monster.

Or, at least, to the mindset that allows things like his Holy Noodleness to even exist.

You see, after I started writing the Quickies series of books, several of my publishers began freaking out. The *titles* of some out my outlined books scared them, and the covers were simply - in their words - "too sexually explicit." Which baffles me, because I've seen more explicit ads, even covers, on some of the girly magazines that I read.

And then they got to some of the content. They were not happy, insisting that I put disclaimer after disclaimer, modify aspects here and there, tweak this, remove that…

My response was the verbal equivalent of the middle finger.

It's simple, really: why shouldn't books be sexy? Sex is a varied, fantastic thing, and what turns one person on may or may not turn on another. But it will definitely turn on some. So why should an author be forced to change what they write, what turns them on?

They shouldn't be.

The kind of mentality that allows things like the Flying Spaghetti Monster to exist is the same that says a book's cover and its content should be bland, stale, and generic.

Think about it.

So I dedicate this book to those publishers, and to those people who comprise those publishers.

And to some of my fellow authors who bend over backward to placate them.

I would rather publish on my own than be anyone's bitch.

Like I said recently in a post online: Bring it. I'm not sorry. It's only going to get worse.

This book, my most lewd and disturbing one in the Quickies series so far, is for you...

Author's Note

Most of my books take place in the same universe (I like to call it the Alexaverse), and contain characters and situations found in other books I've written.

This story, however, does not - it occurs in another world entirely, and is not connected to my other stories in any way.

Because of that, this story stands entirely on its own, and reading anything else is not necessary for its enjoyment.

Happy reading!

Chapter 1

Louis was jacking himself off so fast that Daedre knew it was only a matter of moments before he came. His hand was practically a blur, and his face was screwed up in the goofiest expression she had ever seen him make. She tried to spread her legs just a little bit wider as she played with herself, hiking her dress up with her free hand so he could see her sex without any kind of obstruction.

She had never done anything like this before.

She wanted to orgasm *with* him, so deduced that the best way to accomplish this was to synchronize her movements with his - but it was hard to focus on bringing yourself to orgasm when you had to keep an ear out for your mother at the same time.

True, her mother didn't have much of a reason to come into the barn - she was, after all, cleaning the house - and Daedre herself was supposed to be tending to the various animals across the farm.

Which, in a sense, she was...

She increased the rapidity of her finger movements on her clitoris as Louis increased his stroking and was surprised to feel her body jerk in a miniature orgasm. She was wetter than she had ever been down there, and this knowledge served to excite her even more as she continued to explore her innermost parts with the rest of her fingers. This was not the first time she had pleasured herself, of course, but it was definitely the first time she had done so in front of another person.

It was...

Invigorating.

She could smell the strong, sharp scent of her excited sex, and knew that Louis could too. Knowing this served to turn her on even more, just as it no doubt did to him.

"Are you gonna come yet?" she asked her crush, watching mesmerized as he rapidly stroked his meat, fascinated by it.

In response Louis used his free hand and gently pushed her backward, leaning over her as he continued to masturbate, looking down intently at Daedre's exposed nether regions.

She raised her hands to his chest to stop his advance. "Nuh uh. You can't put it in. I ain't tryin' to get pregnant!"

Louis didn't stop stroking himself - in fact, his masturbation seemed to quicken. "Can uh - ok - can I put it on top of your belly?"

Daedre considered this. She knew she couldn't get pregnant if he put it on top of her, as long as he didn't get any on top of her dress everything should be OK. So she nodded her head, feeling her entire body flush, and quickly pulled her dress even further up so it was just underneath her breast.

"I wanna see em!" Louis said huskily as he used one hand to prop himself up and the other to quicken his stroking.

Daedre pulled her dress up even further, struggling with the large gemmed necklace that her mother gave her when she was just a little girl. It felt uncharacteristically heavy and almost seemed to put up a fight as she pulled her dress over it and, next, her breasts. She even managed to somehow get her hands caught up in it.

She heard Louis cry out and felt his weight drop down on her body, and seconds later felt a sharp, deep sting in-between her legs. He had completely penetrated her, stealing her virginity, something she was trying to save for her marriage bed. Half a second after his brutal invasion she felt spurts of hot wetness being unleashed into her womb. He had pushed his entire length inside of her, and with each spurt she could feel his overly swollen testicles throb and twitch as they emptied themselves of semen.

"Louis!"

She tried to push him off of her, but she couldn't; he had used both of his hands to brace himself, and was lodged deeply - completely - inside of her.

"S-sorry..." he mumbled, not sounding sorry in the least bit.

She knew he wasn't sorry. Even when he was done, he didn't pull out, he just went lax, keeping himself deeply lodged within her, still leaking his baby making juices.

"Daedre?"

Daedre's heart stopped. It was her mother.

In the barn...

Chapter 2

Fortunately for Daedre, she had a little bit of foresight before her and Louis started this little erotic foray. She had found the best hiding place in the barn: a large section of hay, somewhere her mother wouldn't immediately see them. But that could quickly change if her mother came anywhere near where they were.

Louis slowly rolled off of her and tried to pull his pants back up, but Daedre stopped him - it would make far too much noise, and at the moment any kind of sound would likely get her mother's attention.

"Daedre? Are you in here?"

Daedre mentally swore to herself. She could hear her mother walking around the barn, could imagine her looking around, searching, investigating. Why would she think she was in here to begin with?!

Unless she had already checked the rest of the farm first.

Daedre mentally swore again. She hadn't thought about that. Truth be told, she thought her and Louis would be done long before her mother thought to look for her.

Her crush started squirming. She looked at him in confusion and put a single finger in front of her mouth, but the expression on his face told her he was extremely uncomfortable, and being quiet wasn't going to happen.

"I have to pee," he mouthed to her.

She widened her eyes and shook her head, then held her finger up to tell him to wait.

"I can't. I have to pee *now*," he mouthed.

Daedre could hear her mother coming closer. It wouldn't take much to get her attention.

Letting Louis pee was definitely out of the question.

Daedre did the only thing she could think of doing: she bent over and took Louis flaccid member all the way into her mouth.

Louis tried to push her head away, but she swatted at him. She could feel his stomach muscles contract and could sense him trying hard - fighting - to hold his urine.

But he couldn't.

Seconds later his piss was being released into her mouth, and Daedre tried hard not to think about what was happening as she drank it down as quickly as she could.

It was disgustingly salty and strong and came out faster than she thought it would.

When he had finally finished, he let out a small sigh of relief and went limp against the hay. Daedre kept him inside her mouth, waiting for the sounds of her mother leaving the barn.

Instead, she heard her mother doing… something. Organizing things? Cleaning?

After several minutes of waiting, she began to feel Louis' manhood growing erect once again.

She panicked.

Louis reached down and held her head in place as his erection continued to harden, filling her mouth and, eventually, part of her throat. She fought not to gag and was surprised to find it was easier than she thought. Apparently, she didn't have much of a gag reflex, something she hadn't known before.

Of course, she wouldn't have had a way to know – Louis was her first.

She mentally tried to hurry her mother, because the penis in her mouth, while tolerable, was getting increasingly uncomfortable.

Not knowing what else to do, she started suckling it, something that caused Louis' eyes to roll in the back of his head.

For some reason this made her feel even naughtier than she previously had, and she grinned around the meaty appendage in her mouth.

The sounds of her mother moving about the barn receded into the background as she began focusing on messing with Louis, trying things she had never dreamed of doing before.

She pushed her face flush against his pelvis and slid her tongue out, running it underneath his hard-on, managing to get some of his testicles. She moved her hand up to his delicate man-orbs, rolling them gently as she fellated him, and was both surprised and amused when his body responded to her ministrations by letting loose small little twitches. She became so caught up in her games that she squealed in muffled shock as Louis reached down and held her head tight as he shook and ejaculated violently into her mouth.

It was a weird sensation.

When he finally finished, he let her go, and she immediately pulled back and spat his thick milky white juices onto the ground beside her.

She could hear the sounds of her mother finally retreating towards the barn's exit, and closed her eyes in relief.

Then she heard her mother's footsteps stop.

"When you're done, Daedre, please meet me in the kitchen. I need your help with the pie I'm making."

The barn door closed moments later...

Chapter 3

Daedre timidly sat in the kitchen chair as her mother went about getting the necessary ingredients for her famous blackberry pie.

She could feel Louis' semen, mixed with the blood of her virginity, oozing out of her birth canal, and tried to clench her internal muscles to keep it inside instead.

If she kept it inside her, did that mean she was more likely to get pregnant? The thought made her heart thump like a hummingbird's wings in her chest.

She didn't want to be pregnant. She did like Louis, a lot, but she wasn't sure she *loved* him. She highly doubted he would make a good father.

"So who was the boy? Was that Louis, the boy from the next farm over?"

Daedre hung her head. "Yeah. How-how did you know?"

"How did I know it was Louis, or that he was in there to begin with?"

Daedre looked up at her mother and tilted her head, interested in the lack of rage in her mother's voice. "Both."

Her mother smiled. "He's the only boy I know of around your age anywhere near us. And I knew he was in the barn because I saw him sneak in when I was cleaning the front room."

Daedre closed her eyes and shook her head. Stupid. She knew they were there all along. The hiding - and the drinking of his urine - was entirely pointless.

She snapped her eyes open. "Wait, why aren't you mad at me?"

For a long time, her mother said nothing.

"Come here. Beat, crack, and whip these eggs while I form the crust."

Daedre stood up, immediately regretting it; not only did Louis semen (and her virgin blood) begin slowly oozing out of her and down her leg, but her abdomen in general subjected her to a quick burst of pain.

"Was he your first?" her mother asked without looking at her.

She looked at her mother, squinting in pain. "Unintentionally."

Daedre's mother nodded and began to work on the crust.

For a while they said nothing, simply focusing on making the pie.

"Mom?"

"Hmmm?"

"Why aren't you yelling at me right now?"

Her mother laughed lightly. "Do you want me to start yelling at you? Would that make you feel better? I can hardly yell at you when I have done far worse than that, sweetie. I am no hypocrite."

Daedre nodded, focusing on her tasks.

"What kind of- "

"We are not having this conversation, Daedre. Not right now. Now hurry up, I'm almost done with the crust."

Daedre sighed but did as she was told.

For a bit.

"How was your first time? Did it hurt? And was it with my father?" she blurted out, bracing herself for her mother's rage.

Her mother let out a deep breath and stopped prepping the pan, looking down at her hands with an unreadable expression on her face.

An expression she had never seen on her mother's face before.

"Well, you're not a child. I guess I can tell you."

Daedre blinked. Something told her that her mother's first time was going to be an interesting story.

"What I'm about to tell you I've never told another soul. I want this to stay between us. People might find it hard to see me as a respectable alchemist if they knew some of the things I have done."

Daedre nodded. This must be one hell of a story!

"It started when I was just a bit younger than you..."

Chapter 4

My father had died when I was just a little girl; I was so young that I barely remembered him at all. It had always been only my mother and I. Fortunately, we lived a good way away from the city proper - in a cabin out in the woods, in fact - surviving primarily by living off the land. Everything we ate and wore came from the land and the animals around us. We never had a reason to venture out into town, and I had little desire to. From what my mother had told me, there was nothing there for a girl like me anyway.

We lived a peaceful little life in that cabin, just the two of us. It was perfect.

My mother had only one rule: do not enter the forest alone.

It was a rule I had a hard time understanding because the forest absolutely fascinated me. It wasn't that I was naive enough to think it devoid of any danger - I knew that it wasn't. It was full of all manner of strange and fascinating creatures: The Espers, ghost-like fey creatures that were deceptively menacing; the beautiful yet wild wolf-riding Silvestri, and even the occasional bestial Tauron, who looked like a horrid mixture of bull and man. While I knew they were there, I also knew that they lived deeper in the forest than I would ever go and that they were not harmful to Humans by default.

If I was honest with myself, however, I had to admit that I *wanted* to meet something non-human, something completely alien and different than me. As a little girl, my mother used to tell me story upon story of strange and fascinating creatures... now that I was a woman, I wanted to see them for myself. And then there were the various animals, plants, and lakes.... so many beautiful, natural things for me to see. The desire to see them all burned away at my insides the same way a potent alcoholic beverage might, and I finally decided that the next time I got a chance, I would explore it to my heart's content.

So one day, when my mother said she needed some flowers and herbs for some medicine she was concocting, I jumped at the chance to get them.

She agreed, sending me off with the usual warning.

"Don't go too far in the forest. Come back as soon as you get what I need. Don't dawdle."

I agreed, grabbing my basket, and left.

Seconds later I was deep in the woods, farther than I had ever gone before, and quickly became lost. Of course, Aeriel, the god of the sky and travelers, would decide to pick that day to make the sky pregnant with rain.

But I didn't care. In a way, the rain was beneficial to me, for it ensured that I would be unmolested by some of the forests more dangerous creatures.

Or so I thought.

It seemed like I was wandering around for hours. I might have been. Eventually, however, I was found.

Not by monsters.

By bandits...

Chapter 5

Daedre gasped. "Mom! Are you trying to say-"?

"Are you going to listen, or are we going to bake?"

Daedre blinked. "Listen. I'm going to listen. Ma'am."

Daedre's mother nodded.

"As I was saying: I was found by a group of bandits. I didn't know they were bandits, of course, because I had never actually seen a bandit before - but then, except for my father and the occasional villager that came to my mother for various elixirs and potions, I had never seen a man up close before either. So I had no idea what to make of these men.

They had no problem figuring out what to make of me.

They captured me easily and took me to a cave; before I fully realized what they intended to do they had torn my shirt off, exposing my breasts, and I was pushed to the ground, with one holding my hands behind me while the other pushed my skirt up and lowered his pants, exposing his hardness. The other bandits were laughing and joking amongst themselves even as they disrobed, even as the man forcing my legs apart started stroking himself, lowering himself and placing the tip of his engorged manhood to my virginal entrance. I screamed, cried, struggled, but this only seemed to excite the men - especially the one in between my legs. I could feel him moving the tip of his hardness between my lower lips, seeking and finding my entrance and forcing himself inside it with one quick, brutal thrust.

I screamed. It hurt - badly - and my struggling only seemed to amuse the men.

I remembered everything they said. Especially the one who had stolen my virginity.

"Holy shit she's tight! Got ourselves a bona fide virgin here y'all! Well, *was* a virgin!"

The men laughed as if this was the funniest thing they had heard all week.

It probably was.

I cried, begging him to take it out, telling him in gasps how much it hurt, but this only seemed to excite him even more.

He continued to violently piston himself inside me, squeezing my inner thighs hard with an iron-like grip, keeping my legs open wide so that I had no choice but to accept his thrusts.

It was a strange sensation, feeling a man's member moving in and out of me. I had never felt anything like it and had never heard anything about what to expect. I was completely unprepared.

The man humping me shuddered and cried out, and I cried out too as his fingers dug deeper into my legs. Moments later I felt an odd wetness splashing around inside me, and I could feel his engorged member rapidly pulsating, shooting his disgusting baby-making juices.

I was powerless. All I could do was wait until he was finished. He seemed to pour his seed into me for a very long time as if he had been saving it up for years just for this occasion.

When he did finally finish he pulled his spent member out of me, and I could feel his emissions, mixed with my first blood, leaking out of my body.

My crying became sobbing.

It was finally finished.

Or so I thought. As it turns out, it was only just beginning..."

Chapter 6

Daedre was captivated by her mother's story. She wanted to say something comforting because she knew her mother's recollection was painful for her, but she couldn't bring herself to talk - or even move. Without thinking, she reached up and grabbed the necklace her mother had given her long ago, drawing comfort from it. It had always soothed her, and had done so since she was a little girl. Now was no different.

Her mother looked out the nearest window and continued.

"The man that had been holding my arms flipped me over so that I was on my knees, my chest flush against the cave floor. I didn't even have time to wonder what was going to happen next - his hardness quickly pressed at my… anus, and before I could protest, he grunted and forced himself inside.

I wasn't ready for pain on that kind of scale.

I screeched, and his hands painfully dug into my buttocks as he repeatedly and rapidly forced his way in and out of my stomach.

I was crying so hard that it blurred my vision. Even over my sounds of misery, I could still hear the men surrounding me: laughing, drinking, and having all manner of casual conversations as I was being raped. Like this was an everyday thing for them; like my worth as a person was negligible. I was simply a collection of holes to them, little more.

The man thrusting into my bowels did not last long - in a matter of minutes he grabbed my sides painfully and pressed himself flush against my backside, and I felt his man-juices gushing into me.

He pulled out as soon as he was finished, and I immediately felt his emissions leaking out.

I was raped every day - for several days - after that. They put me in all manner of positions to satisfy their lust: standing with my hands against the wall as I was penetrated from behind, on my back as they rutted away in between my legs, and even using my mouth, forcing me to swallow their ejaculations over and over again.

Whenever I objected to one of their requests, something I frequently did as they found new and inventive ways to use my body, they beat me brutally.

However, although I was often beaten, I was not beat; I always kept my eye on the cave's exit and planned my escape in a myriad of ways.

It was only a matter of time, I knew, before they let their guard down. As soon as that happened, I would be gone. That was the only thing that kept me sane.

My hopes of escape were quickly and thoroughly shattered, however..."

Chapter 7

"A slave trader who was apparently on good terms with the bandits stopped by, and the men had little hesitation to sell me to him. Perhaps it was because the slaver was not an ordinary slaver, if such a thing exists, especially since slavery is supposed to be outlawed in our land. No, he was not ordinary; he was an Agari."

Daedre gasped, interrupting her mother's story. "Mom! I thought they only lived in the Wildlands and-"

Her mother silenced her with a look. "Things don't always do what they are supposed to, honey, now do they?"

This caused Daedre to fall silent. She knew exactly what her mother was referring to: she was, after all, just in the barn with Louis doing very un-ladylike things...

Before she could utter an apology, however, her mother continued her story.

"Now as you have probably heard, Agari are very humanlike, save for their massive size, skin color, and mean temperamental dispositions. This Agari made the ones you hear about seem like servants of Angelica, the love goddess. The slavers were quick to agree with whatever terms he dictated.

It was like this that I was sold for a silver coin.

That was all I was worth to them. A single silver coin.

I realized then that I would never see my home - or my mother - again, and that knowledge hurt me worse than anything the bandits had ever done to me. Even as I was placed in a large wagon with several other girls the slaver had collected during his travels, I could not stop crying… and the girls did nothing to comfort me. We were all naked, all alone, and all past the point of return.

We were no longer people, but objects.

And we knew it.

I remember very little of how long we were in that wagon, or of the stops that we took.

I did, however, remember the moons.

They were one of the only things that kept me lucid during our seemingly endless journey in that small, stinking wagon. The moons. Because of the holes in the wagon's covering (which did nothing to keep the rain away from us), I was able to watch them every night before I fell asleep.

The moons...

I had never really noticed them before. I knew they were there, of course, but I had never really *looked* at them.

Nyla. Aylana. They were beautiful. I could see why so many people had written poems and stories about them. I watched them until I fell asleep most nights, their constant and sporadic twinkling barely visible but magical to me nonetheless.

Sometimes I felt as if the goddesses they were said to be were looking down upon me, soothing me, comforting me, telling me in their silent yet magical way that everything was not only going to be all right but also somehow better because of what I was going through.

As it turns out, they were right...

As beautiful and soothing as the dual moons were, however, the three suns were not. They beat down on us ferociously throughout the day, a relentless barrage of heat that seemed to not only ignore the wagons flimsy covering but become magnified by it.

Because of the constant heat, of our sweating, of the proximity of our naked bodies, an undeniable pungent odor began to fill the wagon, lessened only by the sporadic rains. One of the girls ended up dying, and our Agarin slaver callously discarded her body as soon as he was made aware.

He cared nothing for us, for our lives. To him, we were merely wares.

We were truly alone.

Our final stop was a port city. We were quickly sold to a group of sailors about to embark on a long voyage.

I remember the *examination* process well: they had each of us line up on a long table, our legs spread, and examined our sex, looking for signs of damage or looseness. Several girls were turned away, but most were not.

I was one of the ones that were not.

I remember vividly being led onto the ship. It was my first time ever being on one, ever even seeing one, and I was both terrified and fascinated at the same time.

They spent a little time letting us get accustomed to our new home, however, grabbing whichever one of us they fancied using for our intended purposes. Hours after the ship departed from the port we were all placed in cubicles with small mattresses and told to stay there; as the days and nights passed so many different men came and had sex with us that they all kind of just blurred together.

They used us in any manner they wanted, and were all extremely rough – and, even worse, they cared so little for our personal welfare that without fail they each spent themselves inside of us.

It was only a matter of time before we all became pregnant.

And they didn't care.

This thought terrified me. I begged each of them to not finish inside me, begging them to please not get me pregnant, but this impassioned plea only seemed to steel their resolve to do exactly that.

And they were all so violent... often I was brought to the point of fainting before they finally finished.

Yet, not all of them were like this.

Some of them were actually kind.

My favorite of which was a man that I had come to know as Aliest. He was not a sailor like the others, but a practitioner of the Arts, and he would often amuse me with esoteric tales, even show me fascinating magical tricks that most normal mortals would never see.

Of course, he would still occasionally use my body to placate his needs, but I welcomed this, and our joining was more than simply the moving together of bodies; it was a profound, intimate act between two people who genuinely cared for one another.

We were not fucking, in my mind; we were making love.

He was not merely a man to me. And he was more than my lover. He was my best friend, my only friend, and I cared for him far more than I had ever cared for anyone else before him.

And I remember our last time together well.

He came to me and told me that he was needed elsewhere, that he had to deal with a situation that was far more urgent than the petty concerns of sailors. He promised to one day see me again - as a type of collateral, he gave me his favorite necklace, a necklace he had been given by his mother. He said if

I ever wanted to feel close to him, I would only have to hold the necklace, and there I would find his soul.

When he placed the necklace on me, I could immediately feel its magic.

"What does it truly do?" I asked him, the wonder very evident in my voice.

"What makes you think it does anything?" he responded, smirking playfully at me.

I immediately looked at the floor, embarrassed at my assumption. After all, I was little more than a whore, why would an Art user give me anything of actual value?

I remember his response as if he had uttered it yesterday.

He lifted my chin up with his fingers and turned my face until our eyes locked.

"It allows me to always be able to find you, wherever you are. Most people would not be able to feel the subtle yet powerful magic resonating within it. I am very impressed."

I beamed at him, and I vowed then to never take the necklace off.

A vow I kept. Until the day I gave it to you."

Daedre's eyes slowly became huge. She looked down at the necklace that she had been unconsciously gripping as her mother told her of her past, a necklace that her mother had given her back when she was a little girl. It was beautifully crafted, no doubt, but to have once been the property of an Art user... she carefully raised it to her eyes to examine it further.

"Yes," her mother said, turning to her and smiling, "that would be the necklace. You have been wearing the necklace of a powerful Art practitioner since you were a little girl."

Daedre was absolutely speechless.

"I remember well our last night together," her mother continued, "after he had spent himself I grabbed him fiercely, willing every drop of his juices out of his body, praying to all the gods that I knew to let his seed take hold and make me with child. It was a long time before I unlatched my legs from his side and let him go, allowing him to lay down at my side, holding me as he often did.

I felt complete.

Whole.

At peace.

In love.

I knew then that I was in love for the first time in my life.

"I have to go now," he told me eventually, his voice practically dripping with regret. My heart – to be honest, I really can't explain what I was feeling at that exact moment. Hurt is the closest I can come to it.

I am confident he knew this.

"I will find you. I promise," were his last words to me as he kissed me on the lips. He then dissolved into countless colorful, floating bubbles which themselves disintegrated into colorful particles of air, which quickly dissipated into the air around me, becoming invisible.

He was gone.

I held my stomach, closing my eyes and again praying fiercely that his life-giving seed blessed me with child.

I believe the gods heard me.

A short time later I discovered I was pregnant..."

Chapter 8

"Mom!"

"Daedre, you are going to either let me finish my story or we will stop talking and I will never speak of this again."

Daedre was conflicted. There was so much she wanted to say, a hundred questions she wanted to ask. One important question in particular. After much internal warfare, she finally acquiesced and put her hand over her mouth, indicating to her mother that she wouldn't say anything else.

Her mother eyed for a long moment before she continued.

"Once my pregnancy became evident I was taken off the ship at one of the many port cities they stopped at and sold to a place I now know was a *brothel* – which is a place they keep women who have sex with men for money. I didn't realize this at the time, of course, but it was something I quickly discovered.

They put me to work right away. The things I did for the men were not all that different than what I did day in and day out on the ship - except the food in the brothel was better, and the men that came in were quite a bit more creative.

Some were very creative.

It was there that I learned all about *fetishes*. One man, for example, liked to put his member deep into my throat while I sucked as hard as I could until I brought him to orgasm. He would just stand there, unmoving, while I drank his disgustingly salty emissions, his testicles resting on my chin. It was a strange sensation, feeling a set of large hairy testicles rapidly contracting against my chin as they produced the sperm that was being poured down my throat. I would just grab his legs, massaging them in the manner he had instructed me to, waiting for it to all be over with. There was little else I could do.

Others preferred me atop of them, laying back and watching me as I took them inside and rode them, my pregnant belly bouncing ever so slightly as I rode them to orgasm.

I quickly learned that it was far easier on me if these men came quickly, so I learned little tricks to make them do exactly that. Telling them they could come whenever they wanted, asking them if I was too heavy, asking them how my tightness felt to them, kissing them even as I rode them, even as I felt them filling my insides with their semen.

I would ask them if they came a lot, would even take their emissions into my hand as it drained out of me and drink it like it was the sweetest of nectars.

Being a part of a brothel was not all bad, however.

There were several distinct advantages: the food was much better, we were allotted more than enough time to rest, and we were allowed to bathe as often as we wanted.

The bathing was one of my favorite past times - they supplied us with all manner of sweet-smelling soaps and oils, and sometimes I would spend hours just soaking in the baths hot, luxurious waters.

And our clothes were always clean and varying, which was definitely a switch from the ship.

All in all, if it were not for the constant sex on demand, it was much like one would picture a paradise to be.

Then something unexpected happened: the sex slaves rioted and took control of the brothel, disbanding it and killing the owner… and suddenly, I was a free woman.

Something I had not been in a very long time.

I was also a broke woman, however, and there was only one thing I knew how to do to earn money..."

Chapter 9

Daedre was practically dancing in her chair. She wanted to ask so many questions, but she knew if she did her mother would quit telling her story, and she absolutely *had* to know how they wound up here living the life that they did now.

Her mother noticed this, ignored it, and continued.

"Since I did not have money, I had to rely on the lusts of men to obtain it. Looking back, the price I was asking for was overly small, but in my defense, I knew nothing of the business end of such things - that was something I had never been privy to. So I found an old, dirty mattress in an empty alleyway and set up shop, letting men fuck me over and over again, sometimes multiple men at once. Satisfying men like this was not easy: trying to pleasure one with my mouth, another with my hands, all the while keeping my insides contracted while another pistoned himself in and out of me.

Often they would all come at the same time, and that was a bizarre sensation: having a man spurt in my mouth, hand, and womanhood all at the same time.

Meanwhile, my belly became more prominent, making it utterly impossible to hide my pregnancy from anyone. Especially from the men that I pleasured.

It turns out that some men find this a turn on, however. They loved to have me stand as they entered me from behind, some even grabbing my belly as they slammed into me, losing themselves completely over my fat, engorged body.

And then I started lactating and quickly discovered it to be something of a coin magnet. All manner of men loved to drink my breast milk even as they fucked me, even as they came inside me, and it was a disturbing feeling to have a man drink from you and fill you both at the same time.

I would bring them to orgasm in all manner of ways, despite my enormous belly: on top of them, knelt over so they could drink of me; sitting on their lap, draining them even as they drained me.

Some even preferred to suckle on my nipple like a newborn babe as I masturbated them. Their cum was always voluminous, creamy as if they were far more excited and aroused than any of the other men had been.

Finally, however, my body had enough; after one of my customers had finished, giving me the requested copper, my belly started hurting in a manner I had never experienced before, and I cried out for help as I slid down the alleyways walls.

No one came to help me.

Even as I felt my previous customer's semen leaving my body, I felt my lower muscles contracting, and soon I began giving birth..."

Chapter 10

"I had a bit of a revelation after your birth, realizing that what I had been doing was wrong on many levels, and vowed to raise you in a proper way, not on the streets as a prostitute. So I made my way throughout the city, looking for proper employment, and eventually found the ear of an older woman who was acting as the cities herbalist. She taught me everything I knew, and eventually, I took over her trade - and when she passed - her home..."

Daedre's mouth dropped. "You mean, this house-"

Her mother nodded. "Yes. This house, and the farm surrounding it were hers."

"So..." Daedre's mind reeled. She had never even suspected that her mother had been through all that. It was mind-boggling. She slid off her chair and went to her mother, giving her an all-encompassing hug.

"Why are you hugging me?" Her mother asked, a hint of amusement in her voice.

Daedre fought to speak through her tears. "I-I had no idea you went through all of that. I'm so sorry, mother."

Daedre's mother pulled back and smiled at her daughter. "Honey. What, wait, why does your breath smell so foul? What have you been eating?"

Daedre's eye's widened and her face went beet red.

Daedre and her mother both jumped as the door to their tiny home slammed open.

In the doorway, smiling, stood a large imposing man in an even more imposing robe.

Her mother gasped.

Daedre's amulet glowed...

Afterword

The only thing I dislike about my "Quickies" series of stories is the same thing that attracts me to them: they are short.

The stories themselves are fun to write, and it's a nice change of pace to write short creative bursts of freakiness instead of full-blown novels. Not that I'm done with novels entirely (they are still, and always have been, the loves of my life), but short stories are nice.

However, for a person like me, they can also be frustrating.

I like to expand on things, to throw all kinds of various scenarios into my stories. Little things. With Quickies, this is very tricky, and more often than not I have to butcher down what I've written to fall under my 7,500 words constraint. (One of my upcoming Quickies stories, "Cramming Sis!", has a bloody day ahead of it: it's currently sitting at 14,182 words...)

Anyway, after I finish editing and releasing that Quickies story, I'm definitely moving on to a novel - Mya. Where I can make it as long, and as detailed, as I want.

And then it's time for a mini vacation!

*

Now about the world this story takes place in: after some begging, my big brother J.C. finally allowed me to steal the fantasy world he *created*, Zymph, as the setting for this story.

He created Zymph as a backdrop for the Dungeons & Dragons games he runs (which I play almost every weekend -

3.5 forever, bitches!), and he wasn't too excited about me wanting to throw one of my "perv tales" into it. He can be such a girl sometimes.

But, after days of begging, he finally let me, and for that, I owe him big time.

I love you, big brother, for that and so much more.

You will always be the most important man in my life.

Always.

(Now if he'll just let me write one of my erotic stories in his Changed universe...) :-P

Coming Next

Memoirs of a Nymphomaniac

Ellen Parker is a nymphomaniac in the truest, most pure sense of the word...

Yet she didn't start out that way.

In this collection of erotic tales chronicling her life - written by the Ellen Parker herself - learn how she came to be one of the most unapologetically sexually infamous women on the planet, and how this, her first and final attempt at writing, is much more than a simple foray into the literary world of erotica.

It is a final goodbye…

Other Books
by Alexa Nichols

All my books take place in the same universe (I like to call it the Alexaverse), and contain characters and situations found in other books I've written.

The order of the following books indicates the chronological order that the stories were intended to be read in, regardless of series or when they were released. Note that reading in the suggested order will be much more fun than reading them individually, as they each contain references and characters from the books before.

1. Please Don't Get Me Pregnant!

2. Qedesha (Sacred Prostitution)

3. The Champion's Gift (A Qedesha Story)

4. The Qedesha's Handmaiden

5. Taken

6. Programming Sophia

7. Killer Lolis

8. Paying His Debts

9. Knocked Up in Prison!

10. When Daddy Was Away!

11. Voyeur: Season 1

Compilations

About The Author

Alexa Nichols is a full-time writer who loves to write - and read - romance, erotica, and supernatural stories. She draws a lot of inspiration from her hobbies, such as reading, manga, anime, and Dungeons & Dragons, which she's played since she was a little(r) girl. Her main passion is writing, however, and she finds herself doing it (and thinking about it) regularly.

She's also bisexual and is an ardent supporter of lesbian and gay rights. She does tend to lean more towards the females than the males though, so she guesses this makes her lesbianish.

Thank you, **Ronnie Mullins** and **Troy Lake**, for supporting me on my Patreon VIP tier! Much love!